Frère Jacques

by BARBARA HAZEN

illustrated by LILIAN OBLIGADO

J. B. LIPPINCOTT COMPANY

PHILADELPHIA • NEW YORK

U.S. Library of Congress Cataloging in Publication Data

Hazen, Barbara Shook.
  Frère Jacques.

  SUMMARY: A monk's terrible problem of oversleeping, especially when it is his turn to ring the morning bells, is finally solved by a young choir boy. Includes words and music to the song.

[1. Religious life—Fiction. 2. Folk songs] I. Obligado, Lilian, illus. II. Title.
PZ7.H314975Fr   [E]   72-6148

ISBN-0-397-31263-6

for Brack and all our French friends
with love

Long ago in France, in the beautiful rolling hills of Burgundy, there lived a group of monks.

The monks spent their days praising God and doing good works for the glory of the Lord.

The monks did many things. They tilled the fields
and tended the flocks. They read from big books
and sang canticles and chants.

The monks also made fine wine from the grapes that grew in the vineyard surrounding the monastery. Every year the grapes were gathered and pressed in a large wooden tub.

Stepping on the grapes to free their juice was fun. It was one of the favorite tasks of Frère Jacques — Brother John — who was by far the most jolly and roly-poly of all the monks.

Brother John also enjoyed helping the other monks to gather flowers and herbs and mushrooms to use in making medicines to cure the sick.

But sometimes, when the others were working, he couldn't resist a quick nap in the warm sun.

Sleeping was, in fact, one of the things Frère Jacques liked to do most. And this became quite a problem when it was his turn to ring the morning bells.

The morning bells were important, because they began the day for the monks. And each day, a different monk took his turn sending their bim! bam! bom! and ding! dang! dong! down into the valley.

Alas, when it was Frère Jacques' turn, the morning bells were always late—for Brother John was always so sleepy he could not get up on time!

"Something must be done," said Abbot Hugh, who was head of the monastery. And so he called a meeting.

"I have an idea," said Brother Landry, who made the pills and potions. "I will make a strong herb tea the night before it is Brother John's turn to ring the morning bells. It will surely keep him awake all night — and so he will be up in time to wake the others!"

So Brother Landry made the herb tea and Brother John drank a huge goblet of it.

But the next morning, when Brother John finally awoke, the sun was shining and the birds were singing — and the morning bells were late again!

Brother Paul, who was wise and a scholar, and
who wrote beautiful words in the big book,
had another idea.

"If Frère Jacques goes to bed earlier, then he will wake up earlier," Brother Paul said. "And if he wakes up earlier, the morning bells will be on time."

So that evening, Brother John was excused from doing the dishes, and was sent straight to bed after supper.

But the next morning the bees were buzzing and the farmers were busy in the fields long before Frère Jacques shook himself awake. He had never slept so soundly. For the *longer* he slept, the *better* he slept.

And the morning bells had never been so late.

Brother John felt very sad when Abbot Hugh called to him and said, "Brother John, I know you try — but the morning bells *must* ring on time. If you cannot get up on time, I have no choice but to give that task to someone else when it is your turn. I will give you just one more chance. And I sincerely hope you think of some way to wake yourself in the morning."

"I will try," said Brother John. He went to the barnyard to meditate—which means to think very hard —about his terrible problem.

Frère Jacques knelt by a haystack and thought. He thought of the Lord and of the other brothers; of the hens cackling in the barnyard, and of the loud, clear bim! bam! bom! and ding! dang! dong! of the morning bells. But he could not think of a way to get up on time. He was still thinking when he heard a loud "Pssst!" from behind the hay mound. When he looked around, Brother John discovered one of the choir boys, who whispered something in his ear....

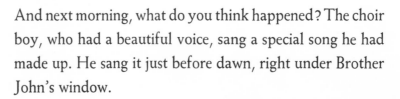

And next morning, what do you think happened? The choir boy, who had a beautiful voice, sang a special song he had made up. He sang it just before dawn, right under Brother John's window.

And Brother John, who had a fine ear for music, leaped out of bed and ran out the door and up to the bell tower.

Then Bim! Bam! Bom! Ding! Dang! Dong! The morning bells rang out loud and clear over the Burgundy countryside.

Ever since that day, the song that woke Frère Jacques has been sung not only in France — but all over the world. And *you* can sing it, in the morning or anytime at all.

English Version

Are you sleep-ing,   are you sleep-ing,

Bro-ther John, bro-ther John, Morn-ing bells are ring-ing,

Frère Jacques

morn-ing bells are ring-ing. Ding, ding, dong; ding, ding, dong.

French Version

Frè-re Jac-ques, Frè-re Jac-ques,

Dor-mez-vous, dor-mez-vous, Son-nez les ma-ti-nes,

son-nez les ma-ti-nes, Din, din, don; din, din, don.

ABOUT THE AUTHOR

Barbara Hazen was born in Dayton, Ohio, and received her B.A. from Smith College and her M.A. from Columbia. Once Poetry Editor of the *Ladies' Home Journal* and many years a children's book editor, Ms. Hazen turned to freelance writing when her son, Brack, was born. Since then she has written dozens of books for children. When not writing, she loves to travel, especially to Paris, and her inspiration for FRÈRE JACQUES comes from her love of France and the French people. The story is a free improvisation on the song, emphasizing the rich spiritual life of the monastery as well as the joyful spirit of the brothers.

ABOUT THE ILLUSTRATOR

Lilian Obligado was born in Buenos Aires, Argentina, and spent her childhood there and in the United States. Granddaughter of one of Argentina's major poets, Ms. Obligado has been a nature enthusiast all her life, and has always enjoyed drawing and painting from nature. She began her illustrating career in New York, and has produced over seventy books for children. She is married, with two children, and currently lives in Paris. The artwork for FRÈRE JACQUES was rendered in felt-tip pen and pencil and is pre-separated. Old churches and monasteries of Burgundy provided background for the story.